ISBN: 978-1-4349-0236-8
Library of Congress Control Number: 2008937112

Printed in the United States of America

First Printing

For more information or to order additional books, please contact:
Dorrance Publishing Co., Inc.
701 Smithfield Street
Pittsburgh, Pennsylvania 15222
U.S.A.
1-800-788-7654
www.dorrancebookstore.com

This book is dedicated
with profound love
to "all" my family,
who have helped
me find my way home.

In the deepest depths of the ocean, down where the coral dances to the rhythm of the water's breath, there was a tiny, hidden village.

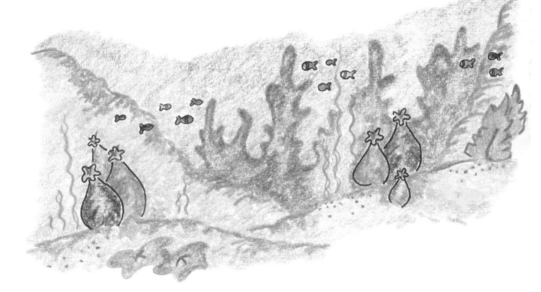

The village was tucked neatly in an
underwater cave.

Now, there were countless sea creatures
that swam around this cave each day.

Some of the creatures were fierce
predators with long jagged teeth; just
looking at them sent shivers to one's
spine. These monstrous creatures were

blinded to the tiny village imbedded
deep within the heart of the cave. What
did live there was a community of playful, rambunctious hermit crabs.

Father Hermit, better known as Papa Crawler, watched over his village each day. He only wanted what was best for his fellow "hermies," but there were two hermit crabs, Harvard and Helena, who were anxious to explore the sea beyond their tiny village cave.

Sometimes, when the village hermies would gather for a seaweed nap, Harvard and Helena would sneak out of the cave only for a second to see the shiny light that illuminated the endless depths of water that kept them from the surface. Eager to feel the light's heat on their shells, Harvard and Helena devised a plan to sneak out of the village and explore the great world Papa Crawler always advised the rest of the hermies to stay clear of.

So, one evening, after a full day of play in Hermit-Ville, while everyone slept, Harvard and Helena scooted out on their own. They carefully clicked their claws past the sleeping Papa Crawler, who seemed to   sleep with one eye opened.

It was a close call. Fortunately, the food sack Helena packed for the journey landed on Harvard's head instead of Papa Crawler's after Helena tripped on the shell of the tiniest hermie of all: Helop. Helop saw Harvard and Helena and carefully crept behind them without their knowing.

As they made their way out of Hermit-Ville, the light seemed to shine like it never had before. Anxious to get to the surface, they leaped atop a family of floating jellyfish who were making their way to the top of the water, but before they could click their claws in excitement, right before their very eyes, coming right at them like a shooting arrow, was a great white shark. Its mouth was wide open, anticipating the crunch of the morsels just moments from his fangs.

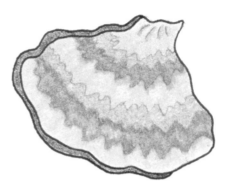

Suddenly, as if out of nowhere, a clam seemed to be hoisted into the jabbering jaws. Helop, small as he may be, had his trusty slingshot, and his first try was a direct hit.

Harvard and Helena were surprised to see Helop, but they were sure thankful as the angry shark struggled to get the clam   from his jaws.

So, Harvard, Helena,
and Helop made
their way to the surface,
breathing a bit more easily
after their scare. They tried
to tell Helop to go back, but he said he
would snitch to Papa Crawler that they
were leaving the cave, so they thought
it best to bring him along. After all,
Helop saved their lives.

19

Suddenly, the light they sought was covered by a tremendous shadow. Fear seemed to come over the three hermies. They all thought in unison, what could it be this time? A sailboat was passing by. Harvard and Helena saw this shadow from down below and now were delighted to see this moving object that seemed to dance upon the waves. In the nick of time, the three jumped on the sailboat and for the first time they felt the wind and warmth of the sun.

As they basked in the newfound glow of the sun's rays, a seagull spotted the three tasty morsels on the deck. As he swooped down for his catch, two little children came running on the deck. Their playful chatter woke Harvard, Helena, and Helop.

As they looked up, they saw the feathered gull plunging toward them, but just as they thought their adventure was coming to a devastating end, the children's eyes discovered the hermies at just the right moment. The children scooped up their new ocean treasures and the seagull flew off rather disgusted.

The children had saved their lives
from the seagull. The world above the
surface was not so easy. The children
took the three hermies and put them in
a glass bowl. Needless to say, Harvard,
Helena, and Helop were not happy.

The children showed their parents what they discovered on their sailboat and much to the hermies delight, the children's parents told the children that it would be best to return the Hermit Crabs back to the sea where they belonged. At first the children refused, but their parents explained to their children the importance of having a place to call home, and if someone is not allowed to return home all those who love them will miss them and be sad. As much as Harvard and Helena were tired of listening to Papa Crawler's rules, they finally understood why he gave them.

When the children were about to throw the three hermies back into the sea from where they came, a tumultuous storm arose. The winds whipped through the waves, tossing the sailboat to and fro. One of the sails had been torn in two, and the ship was out of control.

Harvard, Helena and Helop acted
quickly. They climbed the pole and
grabbed for the torn sail with their
claws. They hung there until the storm
ceased.

Their new friends thanked them as they jumped back into the sea. They waved goodbye, and a little tear fell from each of their eyes. As they turned to make their way home to Hermit-Ville, Papa Crawler was sitting on a large rock that was sticking out from above the ocean's surface.

Harvard, Helena, and Helop swallowed. They thought for sure they were in for a lecture, but instead, Papa Crawler hugged them. He had been watching over them all along. He knew they had to find their way back home, and he was proud of them.

They all joined claws and swam back to the tiny village of Hermit-Ville. It was no longer a tiny, secluded place; it was HOME, and no matter what, no place could ever take the place of home.

The End